Usborne
A Sticker Dolly Story
Christmas Mystery

Zanna Davidson

Illustrated by Katie Wood
Cover illustration by Antonia Miller

Use the stickers to dress the Dollies on the "Meet the Dollies" pages

Meet the Christmas Dollies

Robin, Star and Clara are the "Christmas Dollies." They help to decorate Dolly Town each Christmas, organize Christmas events and are there for Santa whenever he needs help.

Star

is very knowledgeable about all the magical Christmas creatures – from Santa's reindeer to the Christmas elves.

Robin

loves nature. His favorite thing about Christmas is decorating Dolly Town with wreaths and boughs of holly.

Clara

is fantastic at organizing. If there's a party in Dolly Town, then Clara is always the one to organize it – especially at Christmas.

Dolly Town

The Christmas Dollies live in Dolly Town, which is home to all the Dollies. The Dollies work in teams to help those in trouble and are the very best at what they do, whether that's fashion design, ice skating or puppy training. Each day brings with it an exciting new adventure...

The **Shooting Star** train whisks the Dollies away on their missions.

The Dollies love to celebrate at the **Cupcake Café.**

Monique Coco's **Costume Emporium** has everything the Dollies might need.

Animal Sanctuary

Rose Theater

Bluebell Bookshop

Evergreen Sports Arena

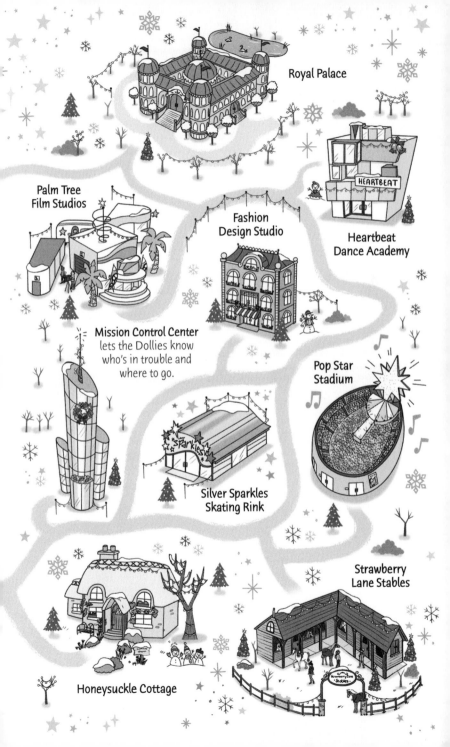

Royal Palace

HEARTBEAT

Heartbeat
Dance Academy

Palm Tree
Film Studios

Fashion
Design Studio

Mission Control Center
lets the Dollies know
who's in trouble and
where to go.

Pop Star
Stadium

Sparkles

Silver Sparkles
Skating Rink

Strawberry
Lane Stables

Honeysuckle Cottage

Chapter One

Snowfall

It was Christmas Eve, and the Christmas Dollies, Clara and Star, were in the Cupcake Café, in their favorite spot next to the fire.

Star was deep in her book, *Magical Creatures of Lapland,* while Clara was checking over her Christmas planning list.

"Oh, just look at Santa's reindeer," said Star, holding up the illustration for Clara to see. "If I had a Christmas wish, it would be to ride on one of Santa's reindeer."

Clara smiled. "*My* wish would be for everything to go perfectly at Monique Coco's Christmas party tonight."

"I'm sure that wish will come true!" said Star. "You've put so much work into the party."

"Thank you," said Clara. "I really hope so." She glanced down at her watch. "I wonder where Robin could be? I'm sure we said we'd meet here at eleven."

"I expect he's checking on the bird feeders," said Star. "After

that hard frost last night, he
probably wants to make sure the
birds have got enough food to last
them through the day."

Even as she spoke, the café door
burst open and in came Robin, a
huge smile on
his face.

"Sorry I'm late!" he said. "I was filling up the bird feeders with nuts and seeds. Have you seen outside? It's just started snowing."

The Christmas Dollies rushed to the window, their faces full of wonder as they watched the gentle drifts of snow falling from the sky.

"Oh! How magical!" said Clara, clapping her hands as the fat flakes began to settle on the tops of the houses.

"We'll be able to build snowmen. And have a white Christmas!"

"Just think," added Robin, "right now Santa's elves will be hard at work, finishing off the last of the Christmas toys…"

"…and tonight," finished Star, "Santa and his reindeer will be racing across the sky."

Robin grinned back at her. "I'm definitely starting to feel Christmassy!" he said.

"This should help keep up your Christmas spirits," said Maya, the Cupcake Café owner, coming over to their table. She was holding a tray, brimming with festive food. There were three hot chocolates, swirling with marshmallows and frothy cream, and a delicious array of rolls and pastries.

"I've brought some of our Christmas treats for you to try," Maya went on. "We've got cinnamon rolls, iced cranberry muffins and our homemade pecan pies."

"Yum," said Clara, breathing in
the scent of freshly baked treats.

These smell delicious.
Thank you, Maya!

Once they were settled, Clara opened up her notebook. "Okay!" she said. "Should we begin our meeting?" She turned to Robin. "How are the Dolly Town Christmas decorations coming along?"

"There's a wreath on every door," said Robin, "and boughs of holly dotted around town, along with sprigs of mistletoe. I checked the Dolly Town

Christmas tree too, just in case any of the ornaments had blown off in last night's wind, and everything's still in place."

"Excellent," said Clara. "And what about the lights?"

"All done," said Star. "As soon as it gets dark, Dolly Town will be sparkling like the night sky. There's a special surprise waiting for everyone at Monique Coco's too."

"So now we just have the Christmas party to look forward to," said Clara. "I've helped Monique Coco organize the food and the music and we've sent out all the invitations. Everyone in Dolly Town will be there. I can't wait!"

Just then, the Christmas Dollies' watches began to flash. Quickly, Clara pressed the flashing symbol on her screen.

"Are you there, Christmas Dollies?" said Mission Control.

"We're all here, Mission Control," Clara replied. "What's happened?"

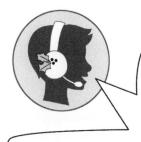

There's a Christmas **EMERGENCY** in Lapland. Someone has broken into Santa's Workshop and ALL the presents have been stolen! The elves have been working so hard to get everything ready, and now the presents have all gone.

"But that's terrible," said Robin. "Who would do such a thing?"

"The elves don't know who it could be," Mission Control continued. "But it's Christmas Eve – they'll never be able to make new presents in time for Christmas Day. They must find the presents before sunset, or Christmas will be ruined. Will you help?"

"Of course," said Star. "We'll do everything we can."

"Thank you, Christmas Dollies,"

said Mission Control. "Sending through the mission details now."

Clara picked up her sparkly-cased screen, just as the mission details flashed up.

MISSION LOCATION:

Lapland

Elf Village

Misty Pines

Search for the Missing Christmas Presents

Top secret mission details:

Find the missing Christmas presents before sunset.

First head to Santa's Christmas Workshop in Lapland.

The elves will meet you there and tell you more about what happened.

Good luck, Christmas Dollies!

SANTA'S ELVES

Small in size

Stocking cap

Pointy ears

Striped leggings

Curly-tipped boots

"Mission received," said Star.

"And please keep this mission secret," said Mission Control. "We don't want people to panic."

"Don't worry. We're on the case," said Robin. "It's Mission Go!"

Chapter Two

To
Lapland

The Christmas Dollies gathered their coats and bags, then hurried out onto the streets. Already, a thin layer of snow lay over Dolly Town, like a sprinkling of sugar.

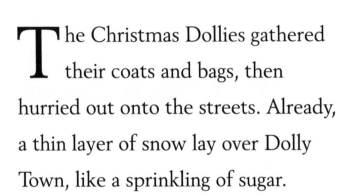

"First stop, Monique Coco's Costume Emporium," said Clara. "We're going to need extra-warm clothes if we're going to Lapland."

The Dollies ran across Dolly Town, past the houses decorated with wreaths and boughs of holly, and past the town Christmas tree shining with decorations.

"Oh wow!" said Star, as they stepped inside Monique Coco's. "Just look at the decorations. Clara, you've done it all beautifully. It looks like a Winter Wonderland."

A huge tree stood in the entrance hall, reaching nearly all the way to the domed ceiling, the staircase spiraling around it like tinsel. There were ice sculpture fountains to drink from, tables laden with food, and beautiful snowflake decorations twirling and sparkling in the air above them, hanging by invisible threads.

"Thank you," said Clara, gazing around. "I just hope we make it back in time for the party…"

When they reached the glass elevator, they all smiled in greeting at Jasper, the elevator attendant.

"Where would you like to go today, Christmas Dollies?" he asked.

The Magical Department Floor, please.

Jasper pressed the button and they whooshed up and up before coming to a stop with a gentle

TING!

"Thank you, Jasper!" said Star, as they hurried out again.

They made their way across
the Magical Department Floor,
its shelves stocked with herbs
and potions, past fairy dresses
and pixie hats, until, at last, they
came to a little door marked
"Christmas Department."

Clara opened the door to
reveal their favorite place of all.
It was like a secret cupboard, but
with doors going off in every
direction, revealing yet more
rooms, full of Christmas treats
and treasures.

"Everything you could ever need to help celebrate Christmas," said a voice, and the Dollies turned to see Monique Coco, gliding towards them. "I know you love it here, but I wasn't expecting to see you until the party tonight. Have you got a new mission?"

"There's a Christmas emergency," explained Star. "We have to go to Lapland. I'm afraid that's all we can tell you, as it's top secret. We'll be needing mission outfits, as quickly as possible."

"Of course," said Monique Coco. "Follow me."

She led the Dollies down a hallway to another room, this one full of winter clothes. At once, two of her assistants appeared, ready to help.

"Now let me see…" said Monique Coco. "Ah yes. I know *exactly* what the three of you need…"

Robin's clothes

Thickly padded
wool coat

Warm fleecy
mittens

Lace-up
hiking boots

Steel-blue
hiking jeans

Star's clothes

Indigo wool gloves

Aqua-green puffer vest

Teal, fleece-lined winter leggings

Hooded, mid-length winter jacket

Warm brown walking boots

Clara's clothes

Extra-thick striped tights

Fleecy, white hooded jacket

Purple wool gloves

Snowflake-patterned skirt

Powder-blue and white snow boots

"Thank you, Monique," said Star, as she handed them their clothes.

"These look wonderfully warm," added Clara. "I can't wait to try them on."

"Neither can I!" said Robin. Then the Dollies stepped into the changing rooms…

When they stepped out again, they were dressed and ready to go.

"Last of all, you'll be needing these…" said Monique Coco. And she handed each of them winter hats, thick and fleecy, and soft as silk to touch. "I've heard Lapland is especially cold this winter, so take care."

"Thank you, Monique," said Clara, as they turned to go. "These are perfect!"

"Good luck on your Christmas mission," Monique called after them.

As soon as they were outside again, Robin tapped the star symbol on his watch. "Time to catch the Shooting Star train," he said.

No sooner had he spoken, than the magical train drew up beside them in a cloud of sparkling dust.

The driver, Sienna, waved at them from the window. She was dressed in a red and green suit, with gleaming gold buttons.

"Where can I take you today, Christmas Dollies?" asked Sienna.

"Lapland please, Sienna," said Star. "Santa's Workshop."

49

The Dollies stepped aboard and the doors gently glided shut behind them. Then the train was off, winding its way through Dolly Town before entering a dark tunnel, glittering with stars.

With a

WHOOSH

it shot out the other side.

The Dollies gasped, for suddenly they were whizzing across an endless snowy landscape. Snowflakes danced across the windowpane, glinting in the low winter sun.

Ahead, they could see majestic snow-clad mountains, rising up before them, the lower slopes covered in forests of fir trees, their branches shrouded in mist.

"Not long now," said Sienna, as they passed through the mountains, and then the train drew to a halt next to a little mound of snow.

"Here we are," said Sienna. "Good luck with your mission!"

As the Shooting Star sped away again, the Dollies looked around in surprise.

"This must be the place," said Robin. "Sienna's never gotten it wrong before…but all I can see is snow?"

The Christmas Dollies looked at the snow-covered slopes, wrapping themselves in their coats, trying to stay warm in the chilly wind.

"Oh look – over there!" said Clara. "I can see a little chimney poking up through the mound of snow. That must be Santa's secret workshop!"

The Dollies hurried around the hill, leaving a trail of footprints in the fluffy snow, and there, sure enough, were narrow steps, carved from ice, leading down to a little door in the snowy bank.

Clara knocked three times.

At once, the door opened, to reveal an elf, dressed all in green, with a long hat and rosy cheeks. But his brow was creased with worry. "Oh! Christmas Dollies!" he said. "Thank goodness you're here! Please come in. My name is Merry. We're so glad to see you."

"We came as soon as we could," said Star, stepping inside, relieved to be out of the cold.

"Please, tell us everything that's happened," said Robin.

"It's so terrible!" Merry exclaimed. "All the Christmas presents are gone. Not one left! We came into work this morning and found they'd VANISHED! What are we going to do?"

"What about Santa?" asked Clara. "Does he know?"

"Santa and Mrs. Claus have gone south to gather the reindeer," Merry explained. "The weather's been so strange this winter – first it was mild and then freezing cold. The ground was covered in a thick layer of ice, and they were worried there wouldn't be enough food for the reindeer, so they took them south to their feeding grounds.

They won't be back until sunset. But by then it will be too late! We have to load up the sleigh today so Santa can leave as soon as night falls. Otherwise, he won't have time to deliver all the presents."

The Dollies looked up, aware that another group of elves behind them had started muttering and whispering. Merry went over to talk to them, and then came back, his face pale. "It's worse than we thought," he said. "It's not just the presents that are missing. So is Plum, our youngest elf!"

Chapter Three

Santa's Workshop

C lara spoke in her calmest voice. "There's no need to panic," she said. "We'll solve this Christmas mystery. We'll start immediately."

She turned to the others. "Whoever took the presents must have left some clues behind. How about you two check the workshop, and I'll look outside?"

"That's an excellent plan," said
Star. She turned back to talk to the
elves. "Can you tell us anything else
that might help us?" she asked gently.
"When did you last see Plum?"

"Not since last night," said Merry.

"She was working late," piped up another elf. "It's her first Christmas in Santa's Workshop, and she wanted to do her best. When we left for the night, she said she was going to stay behind, to finish her toys."

"And where did Plum work?" asked Star.

Merry showed her to Plum's workbench.

"There's a box of beads and buttons all over the floor," said Star.

"It looks to me as if Plum was taken by surprise."

"Come here!" called Robin, suddenly. "The back door to the workshop has been taken clean off its hinges and propped up again. Whoever broke into the workshop must be very big or very strong."

"Aha!" said Star, her eyes lighting up. "Perhaps it was one of Lapland's Magical Creatures." She delved into her bag and brought out her book. "Let's have a look…"

SNOW FAIRY

FROST
FLOOFLES

JACK FROST

SNOW MONSTER

"Jack Frost is always trying to ruin Christmas," said Merry. "But he's away, making blizzards over the Frozen Plains. The Snow Monsters have never seemed interested in Christmas and I don't think it could have been the Snow Fairies or the Frost Floofles – they're much too small!"

Just then, Clara came in from outside, her cheeks pink from the cold. "There's no sign of any tracks, I'm afraid. They must have been covered by the snow."

Merry nodded in reply. "It's been falling all morning," she said.

"But we could look in the Dark Forest?" Clara suggested. "The trees ring all the way around the workshop, so whoever came here last night must have traveled through the forest. I'm hoping the trees will have stopped some of the snow from covering the ground, so there might still be tracks."

"That's a great idea," said Robin.

"Take these to light your way," said Merry, handing them each a glowing lantern.

"Thank you," said Clara. "We'll do our very best to find Plum and your presents!"

We won't let you down.

The Christmas Dollies left the workshop, striding out through the thick snow towards the Dark Forest.

"Hopefully it will be more sheltered under the trees," said Clara. "I do hope we find the tracks soon."

But as they entered the forest, the Dollies were plunged into darkness. "The trees are blocking most of the light," said Star. "It's going to be really hard to see the tracks."

Above them, the boughs of the pine trees creaked eerily in the wind.

"I think we're going to have to
split up to look for the tracks,"
said Clara.

"I'm not sure that's a good idea,"
said Robin. "What if we come across
a Snow Monster or a Frost Giant?"

"Hang on," called out Star, who
had gone a little way ahead. "I think
we're in luck. Come here!"

The others hurried over to look. There, deep in the snow, was an enormous footprint.

Star opened her book. "Look!" she said. "It definitely belongs to a Snow Monster. It's got the same claw marks, and it's the same size…"

"And the footprints are coming from the workshop," added Clara.

"What's this?" said Robin, pointing to a wide trail in the snow, that ran alongside the tracks.

"It looks as if the Snow Monster was dragging something beside it," said Star. "Oh my goodness – what if it was the presents?"

"Now all we have to do is follow the tracks through the forest and find the Snow Monster!" said Robin.

"But those footprints are HUGE," said Clara. "What's going to happen when we *do* find the Snow Monster?"

"And it says here that very little is known about the Monster too," added Star, studying her book again. "This could get dangerous. I know the footprints are our only clues…but do we dare follow them?"

Chapter Four

The Snow Monster

T he Christmas Dollies looked at the huge monster footprint for a moment. They could clearly see five, long sharp claw marks around each paw pad, imprinted in the snow.

Robin gulped. "I don't really like the look of those footprints but we don't have a choice, do we?"

"It's our only lead…" said Clara. "We have to follow them."

"I agree," said Star. "We don't stand any chance of fighting the Snow Monster if it does have the presents. We'll just have to hope we can persuade it…"

So the Dollies held up their lanterns, and followed the tracks through the forest. It was slow going through the thick snow, but at last they came to the end of the trail.

It stopped in front of a huge cave, the entrance blocked by a great slab of gray rock.

If this is where the presents are hidden, there's no way we can get in.

"It looks as if the Snow Monster is *inside* the cave," said Star.

"Well, if we can't get in," said Robin, "we'll have to tempt the Snow Monster to come out."

"Here goes," said Star, nervously. Then she cupped her hands and called out, "Hello! Is anyone there?"

There was no answer.

"We're looking for some missing presents!" she called again. "Please, come out if you're there. We just want to talk to you."

This time there was a...

THUD!

THUD!

THUD!

The ground began to shake and, a moment later, a massive paw pulled back the slab of rock. There stood a Snow Monster, at the mouth of the cave.

The Christmas Dollies gasped and took a step backwards. The Snow Monster wasn't just tall…he was wide too, with gleaming amber eyes. He gave one look at the Dollies and let out a terrifying ROAR!

"Where is Santa?" bellowed the Snow Monster.

The Christmas Dollies stood their ground. "There's no need to shout," said Star, summoning all her courage. "We're very sorry to bother you, but we're looking for some missing presents that were taken from Santa's Workshop. Do you know anything about them?"

"Not only does I knows about those presents," said the Snow Monster, puffing himself up so he looked even bigger. "I gots the presents! I knows EXACTLY where the presents are. But I is not going to tells you where they is until I talks to Santa." He crossed his arms – looking just like a grumpy toddler, thought Clara.

"But you can't talk to Santa," explained Star, careful to keep her voice patient. "He's gone south to gather the reindeer.

And by the time he gets back, it will be too late. The elves need the presents *now*, so they can begin loading up Santa's sleigh."

For a moment, the Snow Monster looked confused, as if he wasn't at all sure what to do. It was then they heard a squeaky little voice, coming from inside the cave.

"The presents are IN HERE!" said the voice.

"Who said that?" asked Robin.

The Snow Monster looked
more confused than ever.

"It's me, Plum!" squeaked the
voice again. "I think I'm in a cave
as my voice is all echoey. All the
presents are here too. But I'm
TRAPPED in a big sack and I
can't get out."

"You must let us into the cave,"
insisted Star. "It's bad enough that
you took the presents, but you
kidnapped an elf as well!"

"I didn't means to take an elf," protested the Snow Monster. "I didn't knows there was one in my sack. I must have scooped her up by mistake." He scratched his chin.

"Come to thinks about it," he went on, "I dids hear a funny squeaking, but I thoughts it was one of the toys." Then he looked down at the Dollies again, fixing them with his big amber eyes. "But elves or no elves, nothing and no ones is leavings my cave until Santa comes."

"But by the time Santa gets back, Christmas will be ruined," said Robin. "He won't be able to deliver the presents on time, and children everywhere will be disappointed. Why are you doing this? Why are you trying to ruin Christmas?"

"I isn't trying to ruin Christmas,"
said the Snow Monster, stamping
his foot in a way that made them all
jump. "I just wants to talks to Santa."

"Hello!" called out Plum. "I'm
still here! Is anyone going to let me
out? And as for you, Mr. Snow
Monster, Santa is *never* going to
want to talk to you after what
you've done."

The Snow Monster bowed his
head, looking defeated. Then he

turned, his shoulders slumped.

"It wasn't meant to be likes this," he said, in a small flat voice.

"Follow me," he said to the Dollies, and beckoned them into his cave.

The Christmas Dollies exchanged glances. "I didn't expect this at all," whispered Clara. "What's going on?"

"I don't know," Star whispered back. "Why would he have taken the presents if he didn't want to ruin Christmas?"

The Dollies entered the cave and there, in the glowing light of their lanterns, was a huge sack of presents, with a little wiggling shape at the top.

The Snow Monster reached down to untie the sack…and out popped a tiny, furious elf.

She stood on top of the presents, her hand on her hip, staring fearlessly up at the Snow Monster.

"I didn't see you!" said the
Snow Monster.

"But you must have *heard* me," said
Plum. "I was shouting to be let out."

"I thoughts you was a squeaky
toy," said the Snow Monster.

"Well you'd better get moving,"
said Plum. "We need to get these
presents back to the workshop as
soon as we can. Santa is not going to
be happy with you. Not happy at all."

The Snow Monster let out a loud
sniff. Looking closely, Star realized
he was crying. A large tear rolled

slowly down his furry white face.

"What's the matter?" Star asked. "Why did you take the presents, if it wasn't to ruin Christmas?"

"I is feeling bads," said the Snow Monster. "I thoughts if I tooks the presents, then Santa would have to let me be helping in the workshop. That's all I wants. Snow Monsters never gets to help at Christmas. It's always the elves. That's not fair."

"But Snow Monsters keep themselves to themselves," said Plum. "Snow Monsters don't care about

Christmas. Everyone knows that."

"Well, *I* is different," said the
Snow Monster. "I loves Christmas
and I wants to help. But now
Santa will never lets me!"

"Why didn't you just ask him?"
said Plum.

"I never thoughts of that," said
the Snow Monster.

Plum wagged her finger at him.
"Instead you came up with a
terrible plan."

"I knows that now," said the
Snow Monster.

"Well," said Clara, "we can still save the day. We just need to act fast and get those presents back."

The Christmas Dollies and Plum looked at the enormous sack.

"And for that," Star told the Snow Monster, "we're going to need your help!"

Chapter Five

Saving
Christmas

"Do you thinks if I takes the presents back, Santa will let me help in his workshop?" asked the Snow Monster, in a small voice.

"I can't promise anything," said Star, gently. "What you did was wrong. But at least this way, we still might be able to save Christmas."

"Then I'll helps!" said the Snow Monster, smiling for the first time. He ran out of the cave, the huge sack of presents slung over his shoulder as if it weighed no more than a feather.

The Dollies and Plum followed
to find the Snow Monster loading
the sack onto an enormous sleigh.
"Yous can ride on here too," he
said. "I'll takes you *all* back to
the workshop."

They climbed aboard, the
Snow Monster picked up the rope

and called out, "Holds tight!"

Then they were off, flying
back through the forest, the trees
flashing before their eyes, snow
spraying up like foamy waves on
either side. The Snow Monster
didn't stop until they reached
the workshop.

"Oh look! Over there!" said Plum, pointing to a low wooden building beyond the workshop. "The reindeer are back in their stalls. That means Santa must be back."

With those words, she leapt off the sleigh and hurried into the workshop, the Christmas Dollies following close behind.

"Santa! Mrs. Claus!" Plum called out, rushing over to greet them.

"I'm so glad you're safe and sound," said Santa, bending down to give Plum a hug, his dark eyes shining with relief. "We've only just returned. Merry and the others were telling us how you'd gone missing along with the presents. We were just coming to look for you."

"It's okay!" said Plum. "The Christmas Dollies came and found me and we've got all the presents. They're outside on the Snow Monster's sleigh."

Then Plum told them everything that had happened.

"Thank you for helping," said Mrs. Claus, beaming at the Christmas Dollies. "Without you, it would have been a Christmas disaster!"

Santa came over and shook their hands. "You've saved Christmas," he said. "We couldn't have done it

without you. Now where is this
Snow Monster? I had better go
and speak to him before we load up
the sleigh."

"We left him outside," said Clara.

When they came out, they could see the sack of presents – but there was no sign of the Snow Monster.

"He was probably too embarrassed to meet you," said Clara. "He did seem very sorry for what he'd done."

"Well, the Snow Monster will have to wait for now," said Santa. "First, we need to load these presents onto my sleigh. It's not long till sunset."

"We'll help!" said the Christmas Dollies.

"Then it's all hands on deck," said Santa.

As the sun slowly set across the horizon, streaking the sky a beautiful pinkish-gray, everyone worked hard to load up the sleigh and harness the reindeer. The sun was finally slipping out of sight when Plum placed the last of the presents onto the back of the sleigh.

"Well done, everyone," said Santa, climbing on board. "We're just in time."

He lifted the reins and called out to his reindeer. They pawed at the ground with their hooves, straining at the reins...but nothing happened. The sleigh didn't move.

"What's wrong?" asked Clara.

"Oh no!" said Mrs. Claus, bending down to look. "The sleigh's stuck fast. It's been so cold the ice has frozen around it."

"We'll have to push," said Robin.

"But we're running out of time," said Mrs. Claus. "It could take us hours to get the sleigh out!"

"Oh no," said Plum. "Christmas is going to be ruined after all."

On hearing Plum's words, some of the elves started crying.

"Wait!" said Star. "I've had an idea. What about the Snow Monster? He can help us!"

"But he's already gone back to the forest," Clara pointed out. "Do we have time to reach him?"

"Take Comet," said Santa. "She's my fastest reindeer."

"Really?" gasped Star, as Santa unhitched Comet from the sleigh. "I've always longed to ride a reindeer."

Star climbed onto the reindeer's soft back and gently pressed down with her heels.

"Away to the forest!" called Santa, and Comet raced off, her delicate hooves dancing over the snow. Star bent low, the wind whistling over her back.

"Good girl," she said, steering Comet between the trees. But she hadn't gone far through the forest when she saw the Snow Monster, sitting on an old tree stump.

"Whoa girl!" she called to Comet, who trotted over to the Snow Monster. "Why did you leave?" Star asked him.

"I was too embarrassed to meet Santa," said the Snow Monster. "I is ashamed at what's I done."

"I thought that might be it," said Star, gently. "But we need your help. The sleigh is stuck fast and we can't move it. Will you come?"

The Snow Monster nodded, and

began running through the forest,
with Star galloping behind.

When the Snow Monster reached
Santa, he hung his head. "I is so sorry
for everything," he said. "I just wants
to be part of Christmas, and to help
in your workshop likes the elves. But
I knows I've ruined that now."

"Well, let's see about that," said
Santa. "First of all, can you move
this sleigh?"

The Snow Monster nodded, eagerly.

Santa hitched Comet to the
sleigh, then turned to the Snow
Monster. "On the count of three,"
he said. "One…two…*three!*"
The Snow Monster leaned down

and pushed the sleigh with all his
might. At the same time, Santa
scattered sparkle dust over his
reindeer. It glittered, gold and
silver in the darkening air.

With a

WHOOSH

the sleigh was free and the reindeer took to the sky.

"Ho, ho, ho!" Santa called out, as he and his reindeer flew in an arc across the stars.

The elves and the Christmas Dollies watched until he vanished from sight.

"That," said Robin, "is truly one of the most magical things I've ever seen!"

"Well done, everyone," said Mrs. Claus. "Now there'll be Christmas presents all round. You made a wonderful team. You included," she said, turning to the Snow Monster.

At that, the Snow Monster's
face broke into a huge smile.

"And now," said Mrs. Claus,
"it's time to celebrate with
Christmas cake and berry juice!"

The elves all gave a loud cheer.

Hooray!

"Will you join us, Christmas Dollies?" asked Mrs. Claus.

"We'd love to," said Clara, checking her watch, "but we've got a party of our own to go to. It's time we went back to Dolly Town!"

Chapter Six

Stars in the Sky

Robin summoned the Shooting Star train and, moments later, it sped into view.

"Hello, Sienna!" said Clara. "Can you take us to Monique Coco's, please?"

Then they all turned to wave to Mrs. Claus and the elves, before climbing aboard.

The Shooting Star wound its
way across Lapland, whooshed
through the glittering tunnel,
and, in what seemed like no
time at all, drew up beside
Monique Coco's.

"Are you coming to the party, too, Sienna?" asked Clara, as the doors opened.

"I wouldn't miss it for the world! I'll see you in there," said Sienna, grinning.

"Oh, Star!" said Clara, gazing up
at Monique Coco's. "Is this your
surprise? This amazing light display?
It's wonderful – there's something
different to spot in every window."

"I wanted each window to look
like a picture in an advent calendar,"
said Star.

"It's perfect," said Robin. "And
can you hear that? Christmas music!"

Tinkling piano notes, laughter
and song wafted out of Monique
Coco's on the crisp night air. "It's
time to join the party!" said Star.

The Christmas Dollies swept in through the revolving door and smiled to see all the other Dollies of Dolly Town. "Look!" said Robin, waving. "There are the Magic Dollies and the Princess Dollies…"

"And I can see the Animal Rescue Dollies and Jasper and Maya…"

They smiled in greeting, as Monique Coco came up to them. "It's a wonderful party," she said. "Everyone's saying how magical it feels. Thank you for all your help organizing it. I was worried you weren't going to make it. How was your mission?"

"Successful," said Clara, grinning. "And," she added, taking in Monique Coco's dress, "I love your outfit."

I designed it myself!

"Now come and join the singing," said Monique Coco. "You deserve this party more than anyone!"

She led them over to the grand piano and the Christmas Dollies stood with the other Dollies, all linking arms as they sang their favorite festive tunes together.

When the singing had finished, and everyone began to eat, Star felt herself drawn to the window. She gazed up at the night sky, then ran over to the other Christmas Dollies.

"Quick!" she said. "Let's go outside for a moment!"

"Why?" laughed Clara, as they followed her out.

"Look!" said Star. And there, in the sky above Dolly Town, was Santa, riding his sleigh across the sky.

They waved up at him and Santa waved right back.

Then behind the sleigh, they
saw a trail of stars, sparkling like
fireworks, spelling out the words…

Thank you, Christmas Dollies!

"Oh, what a perfect start to Christmas," said Robin. "We saved Christmas from a Snow Monster…"

"I got to ride on a reindeer," said Star.

"And we were still able to go to
our Christmas party," added Clara.
They put their arms around
each other.

The End

Join the **Dollies** on
their other adventures.

Edited by Lesley Sims and Stephanie King
Designed by Hannah Cobley and Jacqui Clark
Additional illustrations by Heather Burns

First published in 2021 by Usborne Publishing Ltd., Usborne
House, 83-85 Saffron Hill, London EC1N 8RT England, usborne.
com Copyright © 2021 Usborne Publishing Ltd. The name
Usborne and the Balloon Logo are Trade Marks of Usborne
Publishing Ltd. All rights reserved. No part of this publication
may be reproduced, stored in a retrieval system, or transmitted
in any form or by any means without the prior permission of
Usborne Publishing Ltd. First published in America 2021, AE,
EDC, Tulsa, Oklahoma 74146 usbornebooksandmore.com